To Mum and Dad,
who stopped smoking
~ *J.C.*

To Ruth, with love
~ *B.C.*

LITTLE TIGER PRESS
An imprint of Magi Publications
1 The Coda Centre, 189 Munster Road,
London SW6 6AW
www.littletigerpress.com
This paperback edition published in 2002
First published in Great Britain 2002
Text © 2002 Jane Clarke • Illustrations © 2002 Ben Cort
Jane Clarke and Ben Cort have asserted their rights to
be identified as the author and illustrator of this work
under the Copyright, Designs and Patents Act, 1988.
A CIP catalogue record for this title is available from
the British Library • Printed in Belgium by Proost
All rights reserved • ISBN 1 85430 780 0
1 2 3 4 5 6 7 8 9 10

This Little Tiger book belongs to:

_____

_____

_____

_____

Smoky Dragons

Jane Clarke   Ben Cort

Little Tiger Press

London

The dragons' cave was full of smoke. Dad was smoking, and Ember flapped her wings in frustration. "Dad," Ember said, "have you ever tried to stop?" "Of course not, dear," her father coughed. "Every grown-up dragon smokes."

"Well, I think you should give up. Your teeth are all yellow, you've got bad breath, and our cave stinks of smoke."

"That's exactly the way I like it,"
said Dad. "Dragons *always* smoke."

Ember's little brother Burnie was
playing with his set of model knights.
He loved the way the smoke came
out of his dad's nostrils.

"Look, Dad, Burnie thinks it's cool to smoke!" said Ember.

"So he should! When he grows up, he'll want to be like his dear old dad."

"You wheeze when you fly," Ember said. "You cough all the time. Smoking is bad for you!"

"I've told you," Dad said. "Dragons *always* smoke."

"Ember's right, Puffy dear," said Mum.
She had been sitting on the nest for the last two
hundred years. It was easy to forget she was there.
"Our egg will be hatching soon," Mum continued.
"*Egg Care* says smoking is bad for young
dragons. We must both try to stop."

"Stop smoking? You want me, Smoulder P. Smoke, to stop smoking?" said Dad.

"Yes, Puffy dear," Mum replied, her big emerald eyes twinkling. "For the sake of our children, I do."

"Well, Char my love, if you say so, then I shall try to stop. But it won't be easy. Dragons *always* smoke."

At breakfast time, Ember floated into the kitchen.
"Hey, the smoke is clearing already. Dad, you're
huge! I've never seen all of you before."
"I don't know why you're so cheerful," Dad
said. "Who's eaten all the Knight Krispies?"
"You're very grumpy," said Ember.

"It's hard to stop smoking," Mum sighed.
"It will get easier," Ember said.
"I doubt it," sulked Dad. "Dragons
always smoke."

Dad was hiding in the forest. Clouds of smoke were billowing out between the trees and he didn't notice Ember sneaking up on him.

"Dad!" Ember cried. "You're smoking again! Mum will be cross with you."

"Who, me?" said Dad, trying to flap away the smoke. "I'm sure your mother will understand. Dragons *always* smoke."

"We need something to take our minds off it," said
Mum. "Something nice to chew. Why don't you fly
to the castle and see if they've got any fresh knights?"
"Fresh knights!" squeaked Burnie. "Yummy!"
Dad spread his wings. Ember and Burnie found
it hard to keep up.
"Wow, Dad!" cried Ember. "You're not wheezing!
You can fly really fast when you don't smoke."

"We're in luck," said Dad. "There's been another delivery."
The fresh knights had just arrived at the castle. They hadn't seen a dragon before, so they were very easy to catch.

"Mmmm," said Mum, rubbing her tummy. "Fresh
knights are scrumptious. I couldn't taste them
properly when I was smoking."
"Delicious," agreed Dad. "Crunchy on the outside
and soft and chewy in the middle."
"Oh, Puffy, you've still got the wrappers on!"

"What's that noise?" asked Ember.
"It's Dad eating," said Burnie.
"No. Not the munching, chomping, gulping
noise. The clanging, clattering, trumpeting
noise outside. What's going on?"

Ember stuck her head
out of the cave. "An army of
knights is coming our way!" she yelled.
"Oh goody, seconds!" said Burnie, licking his lips.
"How many?"
"Hundreds!" said Ember. "They look really mean."

"Quick, let's hide!" cried Mum.
The dragons ran all round the cave, flapping their wings wildly.
"I expect they're a teensy bit cross about us eating their friends," Dad said. "They've come to get us!"

"Ssshhh!" whispered Ember.
"They're coming closer."

"We're all going to die!" cried Burnie, trembling from head to tail. "There'll be no dragons left in the world! Dragons will become extinct!" sobbed Mum.

The dragons held their breath.
The knights had stopped outside their cave!
"Can't see any smoke," said the first knight.
"Can't *smell* any smoke," said the second knight.
"Can't hear any coughing," said the third knight.
"There are no dragons living here!" they all said
together. "Dragons *always* smoke!"

Then the army of knights turned and marched back over the hill.
"Phew!" said Dad. "That was close! Just as well we stopped smoking!"

Fire up your imagination with more books from Little Tiger Press

newton
RORY TYGER

Little Bear's Grandad
Nigel Gray
Vanessa Cabban

Fidgety Fish
Ruth Galloway

Fireman PiggyWiggy
Christyan and Diane Fox

Shaggy Dog and the Terrible Itch
David Bedford and Gwyneth Williamson

Big Bear Little Bear
DAVID BEDFORD
JANE CHAPMAN

Is it my turn?
David Bedford and Elaine Field

Alfie and Betty Bug
Amanda Leslie

The Very Noisy Night
Diana Hendry
Jane Chapman

For information regarding any of the above titles or for our catalogue, please contact us:
Little Tiger Press, 1 The Coda Centre, 189 Munster Road, London SW6 6AW, UK
Tel: 020 7385 6333 • Fax: 020 7385 7333 • e-mail: info@littletiger.co.uk • www.littletigerpress.com